"In this striking no'
presents a poignant
falling out, and managing nard trutns.

-K.A. Holt, award-winning author of *BenBee and the Teacher Griefer*

Seeking
Draven

MICHAEL F. STEWART

Red Deer Press

Published in Canada by Red Deer Press,
209 Wicksteed Avenue, Unit 51, Toronto, ON   M4G 0B1.

Published in the United States by Red Deer Press,
60 Leo M Birmingham Pkwy, Ste 107, Brighton, MA 02135.

Red Deer Press acknowledges with thanks the Canada Council for the Arts and the Ontario Arts Council
for their support of our publishing program. We acknowledge the financial support of the Government of
Canada through the Canada Book Fund (CBF) for our publishing activities.

ONTARIO ARTS COUNCIL
CONSEIL DES ARTS DE L'ONTARIO
an Ontario government agency
un organisme du gouvernement de l'Ontario

Canada Council   Conseil des arts
for the Arts   du Canada

Library and Archives Canada Cataloguing in Publication
Title: Seeking Draven / Michael F. Stewart.
Names: Stewart, Michael F., author.
Identifiers: Canadiana 20230591442 | ISBN 9780889957381 (softcover)
Subjects: LCGFT: Novels in verse.
Classification: LCC PS8637.T49467 S44 2024 | DDC jC811/.6—dc23

Publisher Cataloging-in-Publication Data (U.S.)
Names: Stewart, Michael F., author.
Title: Seeking Draven / Michael F. Stewart.
Description: Leaside, Ontario : Red Deer Press, 2024. | Summary: "Ten-year-old Teagan is
heartbroken when her beloved big brother Draven disappears after a fight with their father.
When their father accuses Draven of being a thief, Teagan searches for her brother--and a
way to mend her broken family--using the gift of her father's old, cracked phone" -- Provided
by publisher.
Identifiers: ISBN 978-0-88995-738-1 (paperback)
Subjects: LCSH: Siblings—Juvenile fiction. | Missing children—Juvenile fiction. |
Smartphones—Juvenile fiction. | Dysfunctional families—Juvenile fiction. | BISAC:
JUVENILE FICTION / Family / Siblings.
Classification: LCC PZ7.S849523 S74 2024 | DDC [Fic] | dc23

Edited for the Press by Beverley Brenna
Text and cover design by Tanya Montini
Copyedit by Penny Hozy
Printed in Canada by Copywell

www.reddeerpress.com

To Jilly, Penny, Natasha, and Teagan
—I love you fun guys.

Ba-*DING!*

The Day I Got Lost (1 of 4)

I was hunting.
Late August, a day after rain,
The woods around our cottage popping with mushrooms.
All sorts, for my fungi sketchbook.

> Don't go too far, Dad said.
>
> You're only ten, he said.
>
> Not old enough for *off the path*.
>
> Draven's chopping wood—
>
> Your brother and me both, too busy.

> Yes, I promised.
>
> I'll just stay close.

I was a fungi detective, seeking suspects,
Following the clues like
Who they hung with,
Where they hung out,
When I caught a glimpse of colour,
Like fairy gold.
I hoped it would be
Chanterelles, those tasty trumpets,
Growing under oaks and pines, in groups,
Like families.
I had to check,
And stepped into thorns, picking through to find—
—Nope.
My fairy gold looked just like orange peels.
But there!
A little farther …

I checked.
I *had* to check.
The dark woods weren't so dark   yet.
And I took out my sketchbook.

The Day I Got Lost (2 of 4)

I was drawing
With dirty smudging fingers and charcoal,
A Slippery Jack for my sketchbook with its slimy, sticky cap.
Maybe soon I'd have a whole collection.
I found treasure better
The farther I strayed off the path.
Conks with huge shelves
Great fungi hives
Sketched with quickly itched scritches and scratches,
Loose crosshatches,
Deep in the zone.
Sun through the trees,
Steppingstones of light
Glimmering.

The Day I Got Lost (3 of 4)

The woods lured me.
Drew me into spongy bog with Swamp Beacons
I'd never seen.
I took thick steps,
Leaves rustled lonely, owls woot-wooted
Howling reminded me,
Who else called these woods
Home.

When the trees closed in, mud sucked at my boots,
I stopped—
  Looked for the cottage lights—none.
  Looked for my footprints—gone.
  Fear slithered around my ankles.
 Dad? Draven! DAD!?
I trudged, howling through hooked brambles, lost in dark
Without a clue
How to get
Home.
 Dad? Draven! DAD!?

The Day I Got Lost (4 of 4)

I was crying.
Tears blurring. Branches snatching like fingers.
Swamp stealing my calls,

  DADDY!

Charcoal lost.
Sketchbook lost.
I was so lost.
Growls growing.
Light fading.
A boot stolen.
I imagined a hand having yanked it

       D
       O
       W
       N.

  DAD!

SNAP! Broke a twig, and I froze.
SNAP! Another. Then in a rush, like a bear
Snap-crackity-snap-snap-snap!
Teagan?

  Dad?

Teagan!

  Dad!

Not a bear. Not Dad. Draven.
Smart, strong, safe, sincere—Draven
Smelling of fresh cut wood,
My big brother, campfire warm.

Campfire Warm

That night we had a campfire
Under the stars.
Marshmallows roasting
Two to a stick, chocolate tucked between,
A Draven trick.
Fire ablaze and
Dad smouldering, mad.
>I told you to stay on the path, he said.
Brother defending,
She's back, she's safe, Draven said.
>She could have got lost.
My marshmallow smoked in flames.
But I found her.
>Don't disobey me again.
I stretched toward toasting coals.
She's sorry.
>Teagan—You're standing too close.
Wood hissed and burst,
Sparks showered,
Bit my wrist,
Sending marshmallows flying.
Sorry, Dad, I cried. I'm sorry!
Dad drew three cooling breaths.
>Let's get some ice on that burn.

Teagan's in the House (1 of 3)

Back in town
My house is the place
Where the drum of basketballs beat
The scootch, sweet-touch of soccer kicks boot
And the tap, whap of street hockey sticks slap.
My house is the place
Where the cool kids meet.

Draven has that big-brother grin
That lets me play, tags me in.
He teaches me to throw
And to use my elbow
And that small doesn't mean slow.
        Watch out! Teagan's in the house!

Wanna Bet

My big brother wants to bet.
Bet I'll win, he says.
    Bet I'll kick your butt, I say.
What do I get?
    Can't we just play? I ask.
Naw, it's more fun if there's something on the
                     line ...
                         I don't get what's more fun
                             About paying to play
                                     But
                            Everyone's waiting,
                   Tina, *I'm-gonna-crush-you all*
           And her friend, Amber, in beaded braids, laughing.
    Only if everyone's in, I say.
    You lose to any of us
    And
    You can mop the kitchen floor
    After we mop this court
    With you.
Ohhh! Burn!
Draven's laughter ricochets off the backboard.

The Game

Today we bump.
Bump's a game
Of bumped balls, baskets, and butts.
If I sink my ball before you slam yours
You're out.
My lay up never misses.
    Swish.
It's all net and Tina, *I'm-gonna-crush-you,* is
    Crushed!
Next is Amber with her beaded braids that clackity-click-clack as
Draven bumps her to kingdom come.
    Swish.
    You're gone.
It's just us left. Me and my brother.
But Draven,
Draven taught me.
Knows all the elbows I throw.
Draven isn't afraid to jut his butt and send me laugh-sprawling
onto mine.
Draven can D
        U
        N
        K
        !
Ohhhhh! Eat that, Teagan!
You're on dishes, the rubber gloves are under the
                        sink.

Game Over

Dad bursts from the house, door slamming, crash-rattle-BANG!
Sees me sprawling.

Uh-oh, Dad looks mad.

One word explodes.

D   R   A   V   E   N!

    I'm okay, Dad!
But it's not about me.
What's up, Dad?

        You're a THIEF!
Draven's rumbling replies curl over and under Dad's.
Uh, no—

        You STOLE!
It's not like—
Confusing shouts, obscuring words, making Dad fume.

        You're a CROOK.

...

Choking my thoughts on billows of guesses.

        Don't be a COWARD.
Thief—stole—crook—coward
Each word a punch to my understanding of
Smart, strong, safe, sincere—Draven

        What are you all saying?! I yell.

        What is happening?!
But when the smoke clears Dad falls silent,
Draven leaves us in his exhaust and everyone else goes
Home.

Questions

I ask   what happened.

I ask   where Draven is.

I ask   to talk to him.

I ask   to understand.

But Draven doesn't return.

And he doesn't call.

Dad won't answer

Anything I ask.

I'm not old enough.

So I sneak, and wait, and listen.

Gaps

Draven's eighteen
I'm ten.
Between our ages lies a chasm of
   you're
    not
     old
      enough.
 I'm not old enough
 To watch that show
 To play that game
 To choose where to go
 To be off the path
 To have a phone
 To be left alone
 To know.
 E v e r y t h i n g, pretty much.

Fungal Fear

Fear grows
In the dark
Of my unanswered questions,
Fuelling my frustration.
Fear is a fungal invasion
Chewing, threading, spreading.
Emotions pushing up
That I can't stamp down.
Thief? Coward?
    Naw,
If anyone's a thief, it's Dad,
Stealing
Hope.

Alone

What's the difference, I ask Dad
Between being left alone
And being alone
Because
I've never been more alone
With you home.
Maybe if I had a phone
I wouldn't feel so alone.
So can I?
    Have a phone?
        Of my own?
            Pretty please?
                It would make me happy.
Yes, I'm serious.
I don't say:

                    Maybe if I had a phone
                    I can text Draven
                    Myself.

Teagan's in the House (2 of 3)

Launch pads are built to take the heat
But I am not.
That week
Our house is scorched earth
Where I tiptoe and creep, knowing which boards squeak.
Dishes clink-clank fill the sink and stink.
Nothing grows but dust, must and whiskers on Dad's cheek.
Our house is scorched earth.
I stay small and let Dad sleep.

I Wait

I wait for Dad to find Draven
Like Draven found me the day I got lost
Wandering in the woods
Far from the cottage.
He found me, shuddering and juddering,
Blanketed me with his arms
Told me it was okay
That everything was going to be okay.

I wait for Dad to find Draven
For Dad to be a dad
But he forgets to make dinner
Not even pasta.
I find him, muttering and suffering,
Make my scrawny arms his scarf
Tell him it's okay
That everything is going to be okay.

But I don't know how that's possible.

Missing Draven

Dad sees me slouched, glued to the couch, and asks after everything
I

Love.

    Why aren't you drawing?
I don't wanna draw.
    What about fungi?
Fungi aren't any fun.
    What about soccer?
Draven kicked with me.
    Go shoot some hoops.
Draven—
    Draven. Isn't. Coming. *Home!*

I've got nothing to say to that.
Go still.
Cold.

    I don't know where your brother is.
    I can't find him anywhere.
Police?
    He's eighteen. They'll only search if I charge him with ...
Dad goes quiet but I already know

Thief—stole—crook—coward

But I don't believe it.
Inside me, where it's brittle, something snaps.

Draven found me in the forest, not Dad. Draven.

I decide then and there:

If Dad can't find Draven,
I will.

The Call (1 of 3)

Draven and Dad have one last call.
Words like the sparks
From the cottage campfire
That blistered my skin
Flare in my skull
As I strain to hear, lying with my ear cold on the bedroom floor.
Every spark burning
Conversation surging
Until
    WHACK!
The campfire
    POPS!
In the morning, I find Dad's phone
On the floor
Beneath a dent
In the wall
C r a c k e d
Screen ashen
And
Pretty much
DEAD.

Chopping Wood

I remember Dad's arm around Draven's shoulder
The first time he taught him how to swing the axe,
To keep his legs carefully spread,
Balance the log on its end,
And
Where it should split
With the hit.
When it was Draven's turn,
Lips nervous and thin,
He swung the axe
Cracked the log in half
And Dad said,
       Now you're a man.
How I'd longed for what they had then
Wanted to swing the blade, to split
The look of pride in Dad's eye.
The arm around Draven's shoulder
Around mine.

The Cottage

The cottage is a shack
With walls full of gaps
An outhouse washroom
No running water
Three beds and a campfire.
Almost nothing.

But I wish we were there,
Because

The cottage is wonder
No walls hold me back
A mushroom playground
Running in water
Three amigos, family.
Everything.

                              And I'm going to bring us back.

Types of Detectives

All summer long I was a fungi detective.
I hunted them
On logs
On shores
In the grass.
Poisonous ones
Glowing ones
Wonky ones.
Mushrooms can be tricky to identify.
You need to know
Which ones might grow
On birches or oaks,
Investigate the facts
Look at the gills, stem, ring, and how it's
    Capped.
Maybe I can be a real detective.
Discover what the heck's going on.
Thief? I BUMP the thought   *No way*
Creep past my brother's room,
Wiggle the knob,
Locked.
Sealed.
    Like a crime scene.
Maybe he is a criminal and maybe he isn't,
But a good detective isn't the judge,
A good detective discovers the truth.
Tomorrow I'll learn to pick locks.

Lock Picking Level 1

At school, during recess, I stand and watch my friends on their
phones. Me   alone.
Dad doesn't know what it's like
To be the last
To see.
To be the last
To have this thumb,
This extra limb,
That can connect me to
e v e r y t h i n g,
                    He says, we
                        don't
                            need
                                tails
                            either.
Finally, I ask to borrow my friend's phone
Hamina says I have
            Two minutes
            No more, and to get my own
            Phone.
        Ya, ya, soon.
But soon everyone's gathered around and learning how to pick
locks.
        It's easy, so easy, 30 seconds, the video says.
        Just take your tension wrench and hold it—NOT TOO
            HARD.
        And take your L-Rake—scritchy scratch smooth like this.

It's easy, so easy, if you do it right, all you need is
    everything, and to do it just
    Right ...
I tap the video off and sigh.

    Have you tried a screwdriver? Joachim asks.
And we just stare.

    What? Sometimes I gotto go pee and my brother
        locks me out.
    Sometimes I REALLY gotta go!
    Jab it in and twist.

Lock Picking Level 2

Dad's not quite home, when I tiptoe around
    Creak, creep, sneak.
His workshop's a jumble of sharp and serrated tools,
Smells of woodchips and sawdust.
From a rack I pull—like a sword from a stone—a screwdriver
with a flat head.
I race upstairs, weapon swinging in my hand, heart skittle-
thumping,
Stab my sword in and twist the lock's guts.

Pop!

The door   flies   wide.
    Wheeze! Gasp! Hack! It's like I've sprung a trap!
Big-brother stink: Coughs

out

A little too sweet, a little too sour, like socks that died years ago.
Beyond the smelly defences
        A shiny lacrosse trophy on the shelf
        A BTS poster over the bed
        A camping knife
        A book he loves
        A photo of us fishing.
    Nothing seems out of place.
    Nothing seems out of line.
    Nothing can help me find Draven.
    The trail seems stale.
From the closet topples a lot of STUFF
New stuff I've never seen

Sweet kicks
And flashy watches
Airpods
Who needs five lacrosse sticks?
With the rumble of the garage opening, I shut the door behind me.
Each rattle along my spine a question:

Did Draven steal that STUFF?

Surprise

                TEAGAN!
I jump,
        Dad!?
                COME DOWNSTAIRS!
Caught in the act, I leap,
But
                I did it, he says.
                You did it?

                                        Draven? Is it Draven?

On my father's face is hope
A nightlight in our dark.
                You've been so sad

                                        I correct him in my head
                                                        Mad

        Since Draven went
                                        Since Draven was sent

        You've been so quiet

                                        My mind is screaming

        Since Draven left

                                        Since Draven fled.
On his face is hope. My lips struggle to match.
To smile.
        I have a present.
His hand twitches and guilty-jangles, fumbling in his pocket.
        I fixed the phone.
        It's yours.

                                        It's not Draven.   But,

Really? You're serious?
For me?

A *PHONE!!*

Phone

Phone, phone, ph-ph-phone, PHONE!
I have a phone.
I've wanted this *phorever*.
If fungi spores can be
Cuboid
    Spiny
        Star-shaped
            Jelly-beaned
        Bullet-shaped
Any-shaped
Then
I am **PHONE-SHAPED**.
And   I   am   r e l e a s e d!

Tab

The phone is Dad's old phone.
There's the crack from when he threw it
Like I threw that s'more, at the cottage, when the log popped and
    an ember dropped on my wrist
How my arm jerked
Sticky marshmallow rolling in pine needles and dripped chocolate
    dirt.
My skin angry-blistered
Cracked
Left a scar
Like the skin of the screen.
But I have a *phone*.
    I dub it

        ...

           Tab.

Dad Joke

Dad says,

> Tab's for emergencies. Be careful,
> Phones can be addictive.
> Searching the internet is like
> Picking fungi in the woods
> Colourful, bright on top
> But it goes on beneath
> Along miles of mycelial threads
> That lure you to dark places.
> Mushrooms can kill you
> If you don't know
> What you're eating.

Teagan Joke

My eyes nearly roll right out of my skull.
I say,

> Phones can be protective.
> Searching the internet is like
> Picking 🍄🍄 in the woods
> Shaped weird in balloons, cups, fans
> Destroying Angels, Death Caps, Sickeners, and Poison Pies
> With names like these I'm glad I have Tab
> To tell me which are safe.
> Thanks, Tab.

Mine

My screen reflects my face.
My face disappears when the phone turns on.
I tap my father's passcode out
1–2–3–4–5–6
And change the digits.
Add my thumbprint, its whorls and whirls,
So it will open with five fewer touches when I get a text
From Draven.
I polish the glass
Clean it of all prints but
Mine.
There's nothing I can do about that crack.

When I Was Little (1 of 3)

Last year, when I was little,
Before Tab,
I had a bunny with long ears
Soft grey fur
Sad black eyes
Boneless limbs
That I would wrap and clutch to my chest.
Now 🐰 sits on my shelf
Beside the books Draven
Used to read to help me sleep.

When I Was Little (2 of 3)

Last year, when I was little,
Before Tab,
I had a nightlight shaped like a toadstool.
Its fairy glow would keep me in its ring
Free of monsters.

Topbunking

My room has a bunkbed with a top and a bottom.
When I'm sad I sleep on the bottom,
When I'm very sad I sleep on the trundle bed under that.
I'm topbunking for the first time since Draven fled,
Nearly pressed against the ceiling
With my glow-in-the-dark phone,
Nightlight off.

Draven's the first person I've ever texted.
WooP!

   Hi, it's me, TEAGAN!
I'm still waiting for his reply.

...

Draven's the second person I've ever texted.
WooP!

   Don't be ghosting me,
The third, fourth, fifth, sixth
WooP! WooP!
WooP! WooP!

   It's important.
   You left a hole when you jetted
   A crack in our family.
   Where are you?
   Is the thief part true?

...

I'm waiting

...

Looks like
Draven's not going to be the first person to text me
Back.

Dream Texting

I like the way Tab buzzz-A-zuzzz-A-Zuzzz-A-Zuzzzes
When the alarm rings and it's time to get up.
I imagine Draven texting
    Ba-DING!
I need you.
Fingers dip into pocket, thumb on
Home.
I see Draven's text
And save him
In two seconds flat.
But I'm just
Dreaming.

Belonging

At lunch my friends' ponytails
Wag, wag, wag
as they   s
                c
                r
                o
                l
                l
Now I can stand and
Talk to them
Through Tab
Even though
They're
Right
Next
To
Me.

FOMO (1 of 2)

FOMO means Fear Of Missing Out:
One of the internet codes I've just learned so
I can understand friends texting.
And once I learn all the codes
The screens that kept me out will have to let me in.
I won't miss that chat about that thing
That's going to happen.
Not like last time.
I will be there
Ponytail
Wag, wag, waggin'.

Digital Lie

Tab says ten is not old enough to use social media.
So I tell Tab
I AM.

The Nature of Existence

Now I exist.
My account is private.
No one knows I exist.
I follow friends. Hamina follows me.
I have a follower.
Now I exist.

In the Club

> *High five, Hamina says,*
> *Welcome to the*
> *Club.*

Her feed's full of photos
Smiling, smiling, sun.
She's had a phone
For longer.
I jog to my window,
Drink in the light.

Following IRL

IRL means *In Real Life.*
I've always followed Draven in real life
Ate what he ate
    (except tomatoes)
Bounced the same balls
    (hoop life)
Danced to the same songs
    (Friday night cleaning parties!).
Now,
With Draven gone,
I follow him on my phone,
But his profile is **dark.**
Dead.

Loss Is

In the silent answers to my questions
In the empty space when I need a hand and I stu mble
In the scrabbling of a rat in the walls
Extra chores
One less plate
Clink—rattle—cutlery meals.
Dad jokes that blacken like old fungi.

Tab Joke

Tab promises to fix my hair loss
But it's Dad who is balding.
Tab is learning I exist.

Amazing Awesome Teagan

At breakfast, Tab asks what I like.

Dad says,

> Keep your profile PRIVATE and
> ABOVE ALL
> Don't   be   mean.

Draven ~~says~~ said I don't have a mean bone.

Amazing Awesome Teagan

That's me.

Or will be.

I eat fast so I can sink with Tab into the world of my phone.

Teagan's Snowball

What I like ...
    That's what Tab wants to know
And all the likes that Tab collects
Is a rolling snowball that grows:
The drawings of MC Escher,
The secret love of Jet and Petra,
Pink hair, magic forests, climate justice, and things that hoot,
Spell books, and "the world's largest organism is not what you
    think,"
Soccer and the Top Ten Goals of All Time.
All these things Tab collects,
A rolling ball I like
Watching grow and gaining speed
And the more I like, the more I like my likes, the bigger the
    snowball becomes,
Then smashing down, on it goes
An avalanche of like,
An avalanche of mine,
I crash on, crash on
Down.

Draven's Snowball

Draven's profile is not his only one,
Others are secret, or spam, or "just for fun."
I wonder,
> If Tab can know me
> By my likes
> Can I find Draven
> By his?
I sneak back into Draven's room,
A detective dusting for prints,
Lacrosse—BTS—Camping—Books
That photo of us ... fishing.
I net it all.
Time to go   F
              I
              S
              H
              I
              N   !
                G

When I Was Little (3 of 3)

Last month, when I was little,
Before Tab,
Dad gave me a sketchbook
To replace the one I lost.
A phone is so much better.
It's a 🏰 with so many doors.
High towers.
Dungeons.
Tab lights my way. With its torch.
Tab is nothing like a sketchbook.

Some people like BTS and lacrosse,
Some people like lacrosse and camping,
A few people even like
BTS and camping,
But no one likes all three.
Not one on the entire internet.
I can't find Draven

A n y w h e r e

      w h e r e

      w h e r e

        w h e r e

Seeking Draven (3 of 15)

Draven's old profile stays quiet.
There's a post about the sweet kicks
He bought after the *Lions thrashed the Roos.*
I know he'd be so mad to see
Me search his room again.
But his drawers are full,
The sweet kicks I've seen,
All that expensive STUFF.
Two weeks he's been gone
Two weeks
Missing.
When I find him, the
Teagan will thrash the Draven.

Odd Posts

Draven's older posts are odder
Like he has a code of his own
Posts about *odds*
And

                  S   P   R   E   A   D   S

Odd spreads? Like
    Mango mustard?
    Soccer ketchup?
    Fungi butter?
    Marshmallow mayo?
    Fish jam?
There are *real dogs* and *favourites* and *underdogs*
                         Hamina's dog is my favourite real dog
                         His leg twitches when he gets butt scritches.
Once Draven even shouted *GRAND SALAMI!!*
And
It's a lock!
But I wonder if that lock was easily broken too
    Because
After a *bad-beat* the feed goes
Quiet.
I forage his feeds for clues like I collect mushrooms, uncertain
    which are good,
Seeking the connections between thieves and broken locks, real
    dogs, and salami.
Mostly it makes me hungry for
A sandwich.

Jobs (1 of 2)

Dad tells me to DO THE DISHES, and I
Point to the list on the wall, near the dent, and I
                    SNAP

Teagan's Jobs	**Draven's Jobs**
Mop the floor	Vacuum the stairs
Clean my room	Mow the lawn
Take out garbage	Make three meals
Tidy up	and
	DO THE DISHES

No, I will *not* DO THE DISHES.
Don't you see?! Dad?
Draven does the dishes.
We used to play music and dance.
We'd clean to-ge-ther.
You've sucked up our fun.
You've MOWED down our lives.
Chew on this,
I *hate* you.
    I *hate* you.
        I *hate* you.

                          And

No, I will *not* DO THE DISHES.
It's NOT *my* job.
Draven can do the dishes.
I leave Dad puddled on the floor.
Dishes in the
        sink.

Seeking Draven (4 of 15)

I clean my room
To set the scene
And make a video for Draven.
I dance along with that song we liked cleaning to.
I hope Draven will see it and follow.
A friend likes
My first like.
I've imagined this
Like I've imagined
A first kiss.
I'm happy
For a sec
But they could have hearted,
A like
Feels more like a peck on the cheek
From Dad.

Paying Attention

I click on the video of the girl with the too big eyes.

She sways, snap, snap, snaps.

Her hearts grow to include thousands.

I add a piece of mine.

The clip is fifteen seconds long.

Long enough

For me to realize

With my camera reversed

That my eyes are too

Small.

I didn't know.

    I search for a filter to fix my eyes.

What I know

Here's a list of things only I know
>How I miss my brother and his big-brother hugs
>How I heard the yelling before the throw
>How I am sad and alone.

Here's a list of things only Tab knows I know
>That thing about my eyes
>That MC Escher liked lichen
>That Jet and Petra are just friends
>That I love fungi quite so much
>That I've searched for my brother quite so much
>That Draven was posting in some odd code
>That I've asked Tab how not to be a loser
>And what cute looks like
>And whether I can be mean even though my brother said
>I don't have a mean bone in my body.

This list is growing fast.

Who else knows what Tab knows? Who are they talking to
anyway?

False Start

I wait for the bus
And sketch in my book
—post it as a pic.
Tab approves.
Lichen—close up
Gnarly, flaking scabs
Like the scabs after I was biking so fast
Shoot, zip, floosh,
And couldn't stop
Didn't want to
But—
Blam! Skiddle, road
rash.
That's what Dad called me.
...
I wait for a reply,
Maybe from Draven.
Maybe from anyone.
Heart skiddling
Out of control
Wincing for the *blam!*
...
I delete the post but not before
    Tab suggests
    I follow a man
    who also likes
    🌳🌳🌳

Self Portrait (1 of 9)

  Pay attention, my art teacher says.
He wants us to create something *luminous.*
A self portrait.
We have two weeks to
Set his mind
Ablaze.
  Tab suggests I try playing with matches.

Paying Attention (2 of 13)

At lunch—cheesy pasta—we chit and chat and buzz and bump
with each other
Half on our phones
Half eating.
I wonder what the person behind the avatar of the

Was thinking when they posted that video of the boy falling off
the skateboard.
Looks like it hurt.
The laughter was mean,
But funny too,
When they said that silly meme,
> *Didn't need that spine anyway.*

Paying Attention (3 of 13)

I "lol" the video of the boy falling off the skateboard.
Watch it sixteen times.
Not that I mean to. It keeps looping,
Roll. Jump. Ouch. Laugh.
Roll. Jump. Ouch. Laugh.
While I slurp noodles.
I'm not the only one.
Everyone at my table watches,
Munching, crunching, and lunching.

The boy falling off the skateboard has been viewed eighty-four
  million times.
It's twenty seconds long.
   Hey, check this out ...
I show my friends the math.
   Eighty-four million x twenty seconds.
   That's like 50 years.
   Without sleep.
   Watching a loop.
I wonder whether the person behind the avatar of the
🐱 🦄 👩 knew by posting the video of the boy falling off
the skateboard that we would spend a lifetime watching.

Bake Sale (1 of 3)

At home, I tell Dad
    I need a recipe
    For the bake sale
    To save the planet.
        He says, try Grandpa's Peanut Butter Cookies.
    I say, sorry, they might save the planet, but peanuts WILL kill
Timmy.
        Dad says, try your favourite
Chocolate chip.
    Gooey, yummy, yum-yum YUM!
My phone has two **billion** recipes.
I pick the WORLD'S BEST.

Bake Sale (2 of 3)

The recipe for the WORLD'S BEST Chocolate Chip Cookies
thinks I need to know the story of The world's 🏅 grandma,
and how butter works, and
How apple cider vinegar can remove skin tags,
And to be sure to preheat the oven.
How MC Escher drew mushrooms too,
And the Top Ten ways to keep brown sugar from drying out.
How trees are all connected,
And the trick of warming the milk first.
Avatar generators so that my eyes can be bigger.
I have to know all of this,
And that Jet and Petra were caught kissing.
When all I really need is a cookie recipe
To save the planet.
I click on the avatar generator.

I have a **virus.**

I have an avatar, but I also have a virus.

Someone could have my personal information.

My name.

My birthday.

My location.

But

I'm not old enough to be on social media.

My name is wrong.

My birthday is wrong.

I don't have a credit card.

Or a social insurance number.

Or anything that's interesting to people who make viruses.

I don't care if I have a virus.

I have an avatar

With

Big

Eyes.

Self Portrait (2 of 9)

I'm ready for my self portrait,
Paper and ink
And my Bigger eyes are a better idea.
I draw until
My eyes fill my face
Bigger, bigger, BIGGER!
I make more room for them.
I love my big eyes, even though they crowd out my
Mouth.
If only they were like this
IRL.
Timmy leans over my shoulder
Smelling of peppermint gum, says
    Wow!
    You draw really good
    Aliens.

Scabs

I shouldn't have used my brother's birthdate
But he's been gone since the fight and the CALL.
When Dad was angry.
So *rash*
He threw Tab
Cracked our family
Leaving gnarly, grudgy scabs.

Dad's paler, like he's been kept in the dark.
Not sleeping
Not eating
Not telling

> He says, time for you to go outside
> Baking can wait
> And leave your phone.

I like that

> *My phone.*

But I can't leave Tab alone.
I'll lose the streak Tab wants me to keep.
And Draven might need me.
Maybe he is

> Hanging on the edge of a canyon wall
> Stuck in a falling tree

Or

> Washing out to sea

Is that why he hasn't replied? WooP—

> *You ok?*

Paying Attention

Outside in the park,
There are fewer mushrooms in town but
A birch tree with Shelf Fungi steps looks like a ladder to climb.
I imagine climbing to Draven
Up
   or
      Down
        I post a pic.
            You're streaking! Tab says, then reminds me,
I have to go bake.
Tab knows I like fungi.
That's why I call Tab a
Smart-phone.

Bake Sale (3 of 3)

On the table are the Top Ten Bake Sale Ideas
To save the planet.
Hamina's   🍫 covered pretzels.
Timmy's   🍫 bark.
Joachim's   3D 🦕 cookies.
Rebecca's   icing cream 🍦🍦🍦.
I should have asked Tab and not Dad for ideas.
The internet makes everything better.
My cookies are beside the Rice Krispy squares.
Rice Krispy square boy doesn't have a phone.
Doesn't know better.
Mine sell
Last.

At recess my friends laugh at their phones.
They are on Omingle
Meeting random strangers.
I know what Dad would think.
But it's not like getting into random cars.
The strangers can't hurt us
With our phones between.

Risky Behaviour (2 of 4)

On Omingle
Meeting random strangers
Some are just like us.
    Maybe Draven is there, and we'd be matched by fate!
Some are not like us.
    Like the man who pulls his eyes up
    And makes fun of Rebecca's eyes,
And she laughs,
       But not really.
    Or the man who pulls his pants down
And Hamina throws her phone like it's suddenly too hot,
And we laugh,
       But not really.
I don't Omingle.
I sleep beside Tab.
The screen already cracked
Like a mouth
    For monsters to climb
       Through …

Why (1 of 2)

In class I ask to go to the washroom
And wait for Draven's text.
Beg for him to answer.

I ask Tab everything.
Why am I not happy
Now that I have a phone?
Why do I feel lonely
Now that I have a phone?
Sometimes, while foraging, I'll see a white mushroom
On a patch of black earth,
And I'll wonder, why,
Why just one on all that earth?
I don't understand, but
I know how it feels.
Maybe there are friends for me on
Omingle?
Tab says I should smile.
I take a selfie
And text it to Draven.

Donning Armour

Dad gives me money to buy a phone protector.
A shield for when I am brave enough to set my profile to public
Or I Omingle
And the phone is suddenly too hot
And I throw it.
I buy the red protector like Draven's
And feel safer.

Friend of a Friend (1 of 4)

I take a
> Selfie on the school steps (girl gotta grind)
> Selfie with friends (besties)
> Selfie with Dad (that's his hand)
> Selfie in the mirror (new jeans!)

Friends reply
Ba-D'D'D'DING!
> *You know it*
> *Forever*
> *Lol*
> *So cute. Heart the flowers. (shared!)*

Cute?
I wasn't cute
Until Tab said so
> *Cutie!*

I am Amazing Awesome Teagan!
Ba-DING!
> *Try some makeup*

Who is this ...?
Is a friend-of-a-friend a friend?

I'm paying attention
To a tutorial on how
Makeup makes selfies better.
Stops the shine.
Shine makes flaws bigger.
    Nightmare!
Conceal the ~~lines~~, and
Big   gaping   chasm   pores.
vOLCANIc pimples.
Smooth is hot.
Rugged is Dad.
Big eyes *P O P.*
    Don't have to tell me!
Pluck that unibrow.
    Now I have   *TWO!*
Mirrors lie,
Snap a pic to see truth.
I scroll my library of hideous, nightmare truth.
Why didn't you say anything, Tab?

Friend of a Friend (2 of 4)

I erase my selfies.
> *Try some makeup.*
> *OMG thank you. I will. (follow)*
Friend-of-a-friend follows back!
> Friend!

Self Portrait (3 of 9)

My teacher yells
     W   A   I   T !
Before we continue our self portrait,
Before we can surprise and amaze him,
With eyes as big as his mouth, he says,
        Ideas start revolutions
        Ideas set parliaments alight
        Ideas are best approached at slants
        That's when the glow is buttery
        Art is a metaphor that illuminates
        But you must be prepared to take that L E A P
        The bigger the L E A ... P, the higher the blaze.

Full of It

Bottombunking.
Dad says it's okay to be sad. That he's sad too.
That Draven will come home when he's ready.
Tab says I need to be mindful and grateful and other-ful.
I must be present-ful and enjoy-ful
Every step of the day.

    I'm going pee.

    I'm eating breakfast.

    I like eggs.

WooP!

    Post-a-pic of eggs *(grateful for eggs)*.

Ba-DING!

      Chickens are tortured for those.

I like the reply.

Stare at my eggs.

    So-ful.

      Dad says the chickens don't want them back.

Friend of a Friend (3 of 4)

I have a drawing I want to share
Of fungi fins—it's silly really,
But my friend-of-a-friend is there,
A monster inside my ring.
Maybe I'm not ready really
    To dare.

Dance Dance

I follow the sound of music
Thumping, bumping in the kitchen,
Where Dad washes dishes clink-clank,
Shuffles feet,
Swings arms,
Almost to the beat
Like a dizzy penguin.
　　What's going on?!
Dad grins and wiggles his butt.
　　　　It's a dance party, join in!
His moves are pretty cringe,
　　Yah, hard pass, Dad. You're no Draven.
His grin and the music sputter and dim.

Maybe

Draven's busy.

Maybe

He dropped his phone in the toilet.

Maybe

Aliens ...

Maybe

He doesn't like me.

Tab has 33 reasons why he might not.

I

Download

Omingle.

Self Portrait (4 of 9)

One more week ...!
    I am a thunderstorm
    I am a soccer ball
    I shape myself in clay
But
I look like a potato.
I try abstract,
Divide my head into planes
Like a diamond
Full of faces that reflect
Parts of me.
But
It looks like the soccer field
After playing a game
Chewed up with cleats
In wet Spring.
My art teacher says,
    Trust in the process.
But
My drawing skills,
This thing that I've always done,
Seem to have left
With Draven.

Self Portrait (5 of 9)

I watch my friends, hard at work,
Scritch, rub, scritch, rub, rubbity-rub.
My teacher hates erasers almost as much as phones.
Faces appear on pages everywhere but nothing burning.
The paper lies smooth beneath my palm,
The charcoal powdery between my fingers,
I imagine the blaze having happened
And retell the story with finger ashes:
What is the metaphor of
Me?

I'm super-streaking!
Tab's so proud.
I'm doing it right.
Ten posts in ten days
And to keep it up.
So I do.
Tab's paying attention.
I'm not sure
I could stop paying
If I wanted to.

Checking

I wake and check my texts.
I swipe and check my feed.
I check the time.
I check the weather.
I check email.
Check my texts,
Check my feed,
Check my friends' feeds,
Like, share, reply,
Feed the feed,
Scroll the feed,
Play a game,
Check my texts,
Check my feed,
Check, check, check,
Bang, bang, BANG!
Dad's pounding on my door
      You're late!
I check the time.

                              Oh no.

      Get off your phone. It's an addiction.

                              Really?
                  I want to check ...

Zombie Fungi

There's a type of fungi that turns ants into
Zombies.
Every spore it launches
Every ant it touches
Zombie fungi controls,
    And still it wants more.
When I feed my feed
With every friend I follow
With every like and every share
The phone takes over
Steals my sleep
Steals my time
Forages in parts of my life
For things that it likes
And if I'm not careful
I worry
It'll take over me
Like that zombie fungi.

Addiction (1 of 5)

Is it really an addiction?
Just because I didn't sleep that night
Just because I forgot my homework the other day
Just because I'm behind on my self portrait
Just because I picked up my phone a hundred times and
Didn't
Even
Notice.
Is it really an addiction?
Draven needs me.

Types of addictions include:

Drugs, exercise, food, gambling, shopping, gaming, social
media ...

Are you craving? Not sleeping? Not doing life? Can't stop?

You might have an addiction. And you need HELP.

But

I *can* stop

I *can* sleep

I'm crushing life.

Right?

I think of the STUFF in Draven's closet and wonder ...

Is he addicted to shopping?

But Draven didn't shop.

Thief—stole—crook—coward

Odds—dogs—locks—spreads

I search to break his code

Ah, ha!

Uh, oh.

Oh, no ...

These are terms gamblers use

Even grand salamis ...

Is Draven a gambler?

Wait.

Is my brother addicted? He couldn't be. He's

Smart—strong—safe—sincere—Draven

Right?

Happy Birthday!

It's my internet birthday today.
Everyone wishing me HAPPY BIRTHDAY!
Ba-DING!

      And how old are you?

    Fifteen, I say.

Forty-two people have sent me cakes, party hats, and balloons.
Bloop!   Blang!

    Woot!   Bling!

I don't know who some of them are, but that's a better birthday
    than IRL even if this

Birthday

Isn't

Real

Life.

My teacher tells me to turn my notification sounds
Off.

    Dang.

Happy Birthday, Big Brother
Sorry I stole it, online.
I hope you're
Safe
Happy
And remember me
The sister you used to piggyback.
If you were here
I'd bake you a Top Ten Cake of All Time
And we'd lick the icing from the bowl.
I'd give anything to have you back.
Do you *Omingle?*

FOMO (2 of 2)

I see Timmy's post
About their party.
With their friends
And their presents
And their family
Everyone smiling
Hamina, Joachim, Rebecca smiling
At that thing that was going to happen
In the chat I didn't miss
But still was not invited to.
I would have got them something
About fungi,
    They're big this year,
But I'd rather not have known it happened
At all.

Fungi

At the cottage
We'll search for fungi
Like people search for birds.
Stinkhorn, Medusa, Dead Man's Fingers.
Dad says the internet is like fungi because so
Much of it grows underground and it likes rotten things.
Dad says I'm nonfungible which must mean that none of me is
growing beneath the ground.

that's not how I feel
i feel like teagan
in real life
is just the beginning
and the rest of me is
beneath my screen
including
firefungus
earthstars
charcoal burners
bombmurklas
shootingstars,
two hundred million
luminous
roots going on

and

on

down

.

Self Portrait (6 of 9)

My art teacher takes Tab,
Leaves it in his desk bin of phones that chit and chat and buzz and
bump with each other.
Phones that, he says,

> *Should not be used during class time when you*
> *Should be creating something*
> *Splendiferous.*

I itch to check
If Draven replied
And needs me.
I don't know what to do for my self portrait.
Due in three days.
I draw mushrooms
Which love the dark,
Thrive on rot, and
Are not so
Luminous.
Usually.

Phoneless

My teacher keeps Tab at recess.
We stand in shade, shade is good for screens
And other things.
My friends laugh and share what's on their phones.
Phoneless
I am without, peeking over shoulders to see what everyone else is
    paying attention to.
With nothing to share,
I check my pocket but there's nothing there.

                        What if he won't give Tab back?
                        What if Tab's streak is broken?
              What if people are texting or even calling?

My friends laugh.

                           Are they mocking me?

I fight the urge to
              sHRIE**K!**

Phoneless
With nothing left,
I shuffle and itch and scratch, filling with bitter, **black**
Wait every tick-tock second for the bell to
Ring and save me.

Paying Attention (10 of 13)

I hear the grind of skateboard wheels before the
Kick
    Flip
        Bail
            Ouch
Of the boy falling down the stairs.
I laugh at the boy who falls off the skateboard
And repeat the funny meme,
    Didn't need that spine anyway.
And because
Someone was videoing
And because
That someone puts the video into the video of the boy falling off the
    skateboard that has been viewed
A hundred million times.
And because
The video within the video of the boy falling off the skateboard is a
    big thing.
I
Am
Now
Too.

Paying Attention (11 of 13)

Dad isn't happy.
>He says it was mean
>To laugh at the boy falling off the skateboard
>And why I wouldn't have helped him.
>He says, this is just like your brother.
>You have to control yourself. Take responsibility.

The video of me has over a hundred thousand views.

>>Draven, have you seen?

I tag myself, so everyone knows it's me,
Set my profile to public,
And find many more friends
To pay attention to me.

I text Draven.

My friends say I was trolled
On that post with me dancing to that song we like
To clean to.
Did you see?
Why aren't you here to help me?
You know what trolled means, right?
It's hard to explain.
But remember when you sang for that high school talent
  show? And I said you were good.
What if I had said

      You think you're pretty hot, I bet,
    Like every girl in the whole school is into you, I bet,
      Just because you can lip sync Katy Perry.
            You.
            Are.
            Not.
            Hot.

What if I had said
That
Instead.
You'd be trolled.
What do I do?
Can I still say the word "bet" around you?

Seeking Draven (7 of 15)

When Draven doesn't respond
I delete the post of me dancing.
I worry it means I lose my streak.
Is Draven stuck up now? That's why he doesn't reply? Wasting
all his time gambling?
Don't bet I'll stick around, bro.
I have hundreds of followers. Friends of friends of friends so
Not at all rando,
Just saying.
What does it take to get some attention anyway?

Why (2 of 2)

I ask Tab everything
    Why am I not happy
    Even though I'm internet famous?
    Why do I feel lonely
    Even though I have a thousand friends?
Tab says I should smile.
I take a selfie
And send it to Draven
After the filters.

Seeking Draven (8 of 15)

I ask Dad about my brother and
The CALL.
How I can be *just like him*
And why they aren't
    Talking.
Or even
    Texting.
        Dad says, it's complicated and that I'm too young to
            understand,
        That it's all a little
        Unreal.
        But that it's also all too
        Real.
And I kinda get it,
Understanding is this thing on the tip of my tongue, rumbling to
    erupt, but not quite ready
For release.

The Call (2 of 3)

The CALL that cracked the screen of my phone
Came on a bottombunk night.
Even with pepperoni smile pizza
In my belly,
Legs warm from soccer,
Hair fresh from my shower,
The toadstool light couldn't keep the monsters out.
With Draven missing all week
Dad was already angry when the CALL came.
   Where are you?
I imagined what my brother said,
Only heard Dad's replies,
   Where are you?
      I'm at my friend's.
   Why didn't you call?
      Dad ...
   I've been worried,
      Dad ...
   Up all night.
      There's something I need to say ...
   I'm waiting.
Dad said this like someone bracing for the worst.

The Call (3 of 3)

That night,
My fingers tightened to fists as I imagine the worst.

        I've done something. Please don't be mad.

    I can't promise anything.

        It's a bad thing.

    Of course I'm angry.

        Really bad thing.

    I can't believe you'd do this.

        Really really bad thing.

    Unforgivable.

    Irresponsible.

        I just couldn't …

    There's always a choice to

        Stop!   *STOP!*

After the phone dented the wall,
I shimmied out from my covers,
Pulled out the trundle bed,
Slipped between sheets,
Cool on my legs like diving deep into the lake
At the cottage.

Addiction (3 of 5)

I think about Dad's words, that
>   *There's always a choice to*
>   *Stop!*
But Tab says, addiction's a disease.
I slide down that rabbit hole, learn
Gambling can be compulsive,
Uncontrollable,
Shaming, hidden, destroying,
Unstoppable.
Fear climbs my back
Like zombie fungus.
If Draven is sick,
If he is lost
With a disease,
I need to find him,
Fast.

Addiction (4 of 5)

Addictions make us lie.
They make us falsify.
If addiction made Draven a thief
What is it doing to me?
Have I become that zombie?
Not so Amazing Awesome Teagan, huh?

Responsible

My crying mats bunny's fur, I'm trundling again tonight.
When I said that silly meme
How was I mean
If I don't have that bone?
Which bone is the mean one anyway?
In my arms, bunny crushes to my chest,
Spineless.
What does Draven think of me now?

Risky Behaviour (4 of 4)

My finger hovers over Omingle
But I decide to wait for
Day
Light.

What I Don't Like

Here's what Tab likes that I don't like
  That people like pics of me
that are not really me.
  That I can't stop checking,
for what I am missing.
  That it lures me,
makes me streak.
  Takes bits of my heart
and never gives as many bits back.
  That I looked for the meme
when that boy fell.
  That a screen can bring
monsters into my ring.
  That a thousand friends
cannot replace one brother.
  Still no reply from
Draven.

Paying Attention (12 of 13)

I need a spine when
I tell the boy who fell off his skateboard and whose video of him
    falling has been viewed hundreds of thousands of times,
      That I shouldn't have laughed
      That I shouldn't have shared
      That I shouldn't have commented
      And liked all of the attention
      That I'm sorry.

Paying Attention (13 of 13)

The boy who fell off his skateboard and whose video of him falling
    has been viewed hundreds of thousands of times, says,
    I get it, but it sucks.
    It sucks because I just like to board
    And try new things and that

                means I

                    fall.

And I see how paying attention
Has a co$t.
And I see how we all need a place to play
And that means
    fail.

Post

I post a pic of fungi fins
And before I can delete it,
I have three likes more than I did before.
I post more pics from my sketchbook,
My favourites amongst the flubs and scritches,
The ones between the bungles and scratches.
Gills, skirts, scales, stipes, and spores.
All that is above.
And mycelium, the threads and filaments
All that is below.
   Wow, you're just like
   And this is so
   Have you ever thought of becoming
   Have you seen this
My heart and mind are Ba-D'D'DINGing.

Self Portrait (7 of 9)

My brain is like mushrooms popping after rain
With ideas and connections and cool suggestions
For my self portrait.
Fungi can be parts of me, my
    Woollyfoots
    Turkeytails
    Leafy Brains
    Silver Ears
    Coral Tooths
    Icicle Spines
    Eyelashes
I want to WooP! WooP-it-Up!
Because
    Glorious.
Have you seen? Tab is like my sketchbook.
I show Dad.

Addiction (5 of 5)

My mind is cracking
Fingers itch, itch, itching.
Dad sees my *thousand* followers
My profile set to *public*
That the video of the video of the boy falling off the skateboard has
    hundreds of thousand of views

                    And he steals my phone.
I hope Draven doesn't text and think I don't care when I don't
Reply.

Not Paying Attention

After lunch, in the yard, Timmy throws their phone like it's
    suddenly too hot
And doesn't laugh.
And I see the mean bone
    Could be the phone.
I ask if they want to play
For real.
    Double Dutch, four square, grounders ...?
Timmy squints at me
Doesn't smile or say a word
       Your screen has a crack, Hamina says,
Offering it back.
    Like mine, I say and then, Tag you're IT!
And leap away.
It takes a sec
But then
My friends' smiles all crack
Everyone joining in.

Self Portrait (8 of 9)

Dad returns Tab for the art show
So I can create a portrait of me
My idea
With my head above ground and all Tab's threads of all the pics
    and texts and links and comments
Beneath.
I call it. *My Cell I am.*
    Get it? *Mycelium.*
Ba-DING!
It takes me all day
My teacher calls it *victorious.*

I pin my portrait to my feed
Ba-DING!
Friend of a friend posts their fun fun reply
I go cold like I did when I fell off my bike
And didn't know how bad the rash would be,

>*What are you, like ten?*

I stare at my screen, ready to like
Someone paying attention to me.
Then I smile.
I giggle,
And laugh,
Because the joke's on them.

>*Maybe I am,*

I say,
As I unfollow
And **BLOCK** them
Phorever.

Seeking Draven (9 of 15)

As I look at my art
And I look at Draven's lack of replies,
I realize,
If I'm a mushroom, then Draven must be too,
Hiding in the dark but connected and connecting.
I seek out his friends, their public profiles and busy feeds,
It's like looking in stumps, under logs, along trunks, and in the
trees, until
  There, I find him
Draven, smiling, at a friend.

I track the tag to
Lacrossemaster964, set to private
His profile pic, the shiny trophy top.
    Are you my brother?
He follows me, and a chill slides down my spine.
    Are you ok?
    What happened?
A direct message, so he can *really* talk.
At least he's fast
I played with fire.
    What happened? I ask.
You're too young to get it.
I have a phone now, I say,
Itching the scar on my wrist.
You can't help with something like this.
    Why not give me a try?
No.
    No? Are you gambling?
    ...
    Do you need help?
Just leave me
ALONE.
My world shrinks by a brother.

ALONE

ALLCAPS is a shout
That
Feels like a slap
A blistering burn
A fall from a bike
A jut of a butt that shoves me away
From the one thing I want.
ALLCAPS   *ALONE*
Is not the Draven
I remember.
That let me play, tagged me in.
My heart bleeds like my knee had,
Face turned away,
Hot from the loss of my big-brother's grin.
But then
Draven likes my self portrait.
...
A like is not a hug
Or an answer
But
It *is* a poke.

Self Portrait (9 of 9)

That night I show Dad my self portrait.
His eyes blur.

> He says there's more to me than he realized.
> That I'm older. Maturing.
> He's sorry
> About being angry.
> And he says, he's glad I used the phone like this, as a tool
> > like a thumb.
> I say, it's okay. He's really a *fun guy*.
> Get it? *Fungi.*
> Ba-DING!

He stops laughing when I ask
Again
About that CALL
And
The gambling.

S l o w l y
Dad explains
How my brother *had* been   gambling
On the internet.
How it hadn't seemed   real
How he'd thought he'd
Get it ALL   back
If he just kept playing.

Dad says that the money is real and the people calling him
are real.

The

Rash

Is

Real.

And
Poff, piff, p a f f

That understanding that was on the tip of my tongue, rumbling to
erupt, but not quite ready

For release

That thing billows   OUT.

I grab Dad's sleeve and jerk it up and down.

    This is like

    Fungi

    Small above,

    Big below.

    Or my streak, how I could have STOPPED   but didn't.

    How ten followers weren't enough, not a hundred, not even a
        thousand,

    And how when I laughed at that boy falling off the skateboard,
        I was just doing what people had seen a hundred million
        times.

I tell him not to be **angry** at my brother
Because the internet is made this way,
To confuse what's real and not,
And to forget about the co$t
Of paying attention.
At all co$t,
To keep playing.
But that parts of the internet are beautiful too
    Luminous, splendiferous, glorious.
Some is edible, some is not,
But we need a chance to know which is which
And need help when we can't ... stop.
Compulsive, uncontrollable, destroying
It *is* addicting.
It can be an illness.
And if Draven's addicted,
Draven needs help, not
Rage.

Seeking Draven (15 of 15)

Dad puts his head in his hands and his fingers through the last bit
    of the hair his phone couldn't help him with, and he
Nods.
    Let's text Draven to see how we can help.
He nods, but then
He shakes his head—doesn't know how to reach him.
    But I can help with that.
Surprised, Dad's eyes shine,
With the look of pride I longed for, and
He throws his arms around me.
Funny how I long for the arms around my neck, now to be
Around Draven's too.
After Dad texts Draven
    I suggest a phone free night
And I turn on some music
A hip-hop beat
That Draven would like.
Dad cocks his head
As I hold out my hand.
    Dad says, I'm no Draven.
    No, but you *can* dance like Dad.

Draven's Reply to Me

I'm so embarrassed ...
I do need help.
I've tried to stop.
It's hard to say
How it all started.
An ad for a book, I've always liked books, but this one could
    make a lot of money.
This book had no pages,
Just lists of bets I could make
To make a lot of money.
It was exciting to win
First twenty, then fifty, then a *hundred*.
It was hard to see anything was wrong
When I was flush and could buy whatever I wanted after I won a
    THOUSAND DOLLARS CASH.
Felt like playing lacrosse,
The ball thwacking the back of the net,
The roar of my team as I scored.
But the bets grew bigger,
The bets grew riskier,
And the bigger they got the more I los

                t

I'd lost my touch, shots going   wide.
I had to keep playing at any cost.
I couldn't sleep.
I couldn't eat.
I was so lost.

The only fun I had was with you.
I stole Dad's credit card
To make a bet that was a *sure thing*
That could pay my debts.
One last bet.
But there's no such thing as a sure thing in gambling,
And when Dad discovered I'd taken his card,
I was too deep in,
I'd ruined my life and yours too,
So I fled.
I've been trying to stop ...
All your texts
All your posts
They helped keep me trying,
Until
Dad's message tapped me on the   shoulder.

Emergency

Sorry Dad
It's an emergency, I text.
I see now that this has been hard for you too.
Lonely.
So –
I love you.
Wanted you to know.
A minute later, he replies.
A text like Grandpa's cookies taste
And I text back
linking my brother in
Mycelial threads
Chatting.
Maybe
A family is like fungi, too.

Help

Help takes   T
       E   I
         M
Addiction wants Draven's attention
And he's still paying.
Draven has his big-brother grin,
But I am slower to hug.
He's not only *smart–strong–safe–sincere—Draven,*
His head hangs hard with the weight.
Maybe he is the Draven I knew, I just didn't see
The miles of mycelial threads beneath.
I try to fully love what I can't fully trust.
Trust takes T
      E   I
       M
Too.

Draven's job is to sell the STUFF to pay part of the bill,
And attend the sessions that will help him s l o w l y recover.
Dad's job is to tell Draven he's not responsible for being ill.
My job is to distract Draven when his eyes skitter-scramble for
    escape.

    Wanna play bump? I ask.
You bet.
We all freeze
 —and he shuts his eyes as if holding pain—sobs—breath back—
Yes, I mean, YES!

    Watch out! Teagan's in the house!

Teagan's in the House (3 of 3)

Our house is *the* place
Where we bop-pop to the hip-hop,
We shoot, slap, and boot until we droop,
And we struggle, muddle, and sometimes fail.
Our house is the place
Where we get back on our feet.

Nonfungible Teagan

That night in my bunk,
Bunny at my side,
Toadstool *luminous,*
I change my avatar to a mushroom,
And my profile to Nonfungible Teagan.
Dad explained that nonfungible really means not exchangeable,
Unique.
I think of the Top Ten Things to do at the cottage
Next summer with Draven.
Then I delete
Omingle
From my phone
Phorever.

*If you, or anyone you know, might be suffering
from an addiction, talk to a trusted adult
or call, text, or chat with:
Canada: www.kidshelpphone.ca
1-800-668-6868 or text 686868
USA: www.crisistextline.org
Text HOME to 741741*

Acknowledgments

The creation of a book is like fungi too. I owe a great deal to a
fabulous network of people.

To Holly Doll, my copyeditor Penny, and to the marketing and sales
team at Red Deer Press and Fitzhenry & Whiteside, thank you
for helping launch this into the world.

To Beverley Brenna who saw in a little book a spark of something
and stoked that fire, again and again and again until it popped,
thank you for your care and genius.

To Kari Anne Holt who changed my life forever when she handed
me Love That Dog and told me I could do this too. Well, I
certainly didn't do it alone, but we did it.

To Brianna Jett, who responded to a poetry emergency with her
brilliance, her generosity, and her encouraging critique.

To Catherine Michele Adams who has been with me from the very
very beginning, when I was just a writing spore.

To Dr. Michelle Hagerman for your huge reservoir of knowledge
and sense of fun and diligence in crafting the Teacher's
Resource, you have grown the value of this book seven fold.

To the VCFA Writing for Children and Young Adults community,
my fellow Kind-Read Spirits, and to the Sunnyside Writers
Group, you are my mycelium.

To Andrea, mother tree and love of my life, and to my daughters,
Teagan, Natasha, Penny, and Jilly. I love all my button
mushrooms so so much.

Thank you one and all.

Author Interview

What first drew you to tell Teagan's story in free verse...?
The inspiration to work in verse came from reading the work of
two authors. Sharon Creech wrote *Love That Dog* and I encourage
everyone to go out and grab a copy. This book did for a middle-aged
author what it was designed to do for a young student—showed me
I could write poetry, too. Secondly, the books of KA Holt, whom I
consider a genius of the form. Kari Anne showed me how fun it can
be. It was with Kari Anne that this story began.

**You have developed a character here who displays an
indepth knowledge of fungi—is this an interest of yours?**
I love all that is weird and interesting, but the fungi really stems from
my daughter's passion—that love goes DEEP. Every hike has since
become a treasure hunt. Once the metaphor comparing the internet
and fungal networks was established, it was unstoppable, threading
its way into all aspects of the story.

**The verse novel form has appeared as a rising star in books
for contemporary young people. Why did you select free
verse as the vehicle to tell Teagan's story?**
This story is about Teagan's learning to become digitally resilient,
and I wanted the form to reflect that. Verse has more in common
with the internet than prose does. The internet has more freedom of
the page, reading quite differently whether it be a text, or threaded
post, or a long scrolling blog. I wanted Teagan as a newcomer to the
internet to occupy this world. Verse echoes the internet's form and
allows me to explore it visually.

Why was the digital world an important setting to include in this story about Teagan and her family?

I have four daughters and I see firsthand their challenges navigating technology. I think it's important for stories to include the digital landscape because that is where much of their lives takes place. Phones can feel like limbs, beloved pets, or even a little like Gollum's precious ring in *The Lord of the Rings*. Technology is entirely embedded in the lives of our children, it's not separate, rather integrated and part of their identity, social structures, future work, and relationships. We need to have these conversations, and I hope the novel and Teacher's Resource helps facilitate these discussions.

You have an amazing track record of published writing— over two dozen books for kids and young adults. What advice do you have for other writers? What's kept you going through so many projects?

I can't stress enough the importance of reading. Read with an eye to craft. Other authors can teach us a great deal. They can inspire. As for what's kept me going, the urge to write is not something I've been able to turn off. At any time, I have three other projects I can't wait to work on simmering in the skull-cauldron. These are books that I hope can make real differences in the hands of kids. Ultimately that's why I keep writing.

As someone who studied creative writing at the masters' level, what can be learned by formal higher education for writers?

I decided to take my master's when I felt my writing had plateaued. My books, although outwardly different, felt similar to me in terms of calibre. I needed help. The master's programme pushed me to experiment, broke past a number of self imposed limitations, and then showed me how to continue to teach myself. That's the true gift of it. It has touched every aspect of my practice.

How has writing this verse novel intrigued you? Challenged you? Changed you?

For me, writing in verse is entirely different than writing in prose. It requires a different part of my brain. With prose I may start a chapter considering a character's goal, the obstacle they face, the tactic they intend to use to surmount it, etc. Verse begins with emotion. What emotion do I hope to convey? What words convey that emotion? Which of these words evoke the setting? Which of these words would my character choose? It's like creating a new recipe for an unknown pie starting with the spices, and then adding the wet, and then the dry, hoping the whole thing will stick together in the end. Somehow, magically, it sometimes does! Writing verse has taught me to embrace this magic. To experiment and play.